Ransom Neutron Stars
Fit for Love
by Elizabeth Dale
Illustrated by Mark Long

Published by Ransom Publishing Ltd.
Unit 7, Brocklands Farm, West Meon, Hampshire GU32 1JN, UK
www.ransom.co.uk

ISBN   978 178591 441 6
First published in 2017

Fit for Love

Elizabeth Dale

Illustrated by Mark Long

Lisa ran along the street.

She was out of puff.

"I must get fit," she said to herself.

Suddenly Lisa tripped on the kerb.

She fell over.

She lay on the pavement.

"Let me help you," said a man.

Lisa looked at the man.

Her legs went all wobbly. The man was a hunk!

Lisa fancied him.

"I'm Guy," he said.

"I'm Lisa," Lisa said.

"I'll jog with you," Guy said.

Lisa jogged with Guy, but her leg hurt.

"Poor you," Guy said. "Let's go jogging next week. I will run with you. I want to get fit, too."

Guy was hot.

"Yes!" Lisa said. "Let's go jogging on Tuesday!"

On Tuesday, Guy and Lisa went jogging.

Guy was a fast runner.

Lisa fell over again.

"It's OK," Guy said. "We can get fit at the gym. Let's go on Thursday."

On Thursday, Guy and Lisa went
to the gym.

They had a coffee and chatted.

Guy and Lisa liked the same films and the same music.

They chatted all afternoon.

It was too late to get fit today!

"Oh dear," Guy said. "Let's come back tomorrow. We can get fit then."

"Guy," Lisa said, "I don't like jogging. I don't like getting fit."

"I hate jogging too!" Guy said. "You were jogging when I met you. I just wanted to see you again."

"I wasn't jogging," Lisa said. "I was running for the bus!"

"Let's go and see a film," Guy said.

CINEMA